THE

CATASTROPHIC

ORDEALS

NOAH NICHOLAS MWANAKA

COPYRIGHT

No part of this book may be used or reproduced by any means, graphic, electronic or mechanical, including photocopying, recording, taping or by any information, storage retrieval system without the written permission of the Publisher, and Author, Noah Nicholas Mwanaka. This book can be ordered through online booksellers.

ISBN 9781738733439

DEDICATION

Grief-stricken, I dedicate this book to the innocent people of the WORLD who underwent torture, anguish, inhumanity or death for the crimes they never committed.

The CATASTROPHIC ORDEALS is an explosive, harrowing and atrocious story about a man who was alleged to have caused the deaths of more than a hundred people. He underwent a draconian trial, and was sentenced to death for a crime he never committed. Then subsequently, at gunpoint, he was forced to dig his own grave.

TABLE OF CONTENTS

CHAPTER 1

Fervently I had colluded with an insurgent force which aimed at overthrowing the colonial Rhodesian government. Shortly after a gory attack on a regime camp the resistance fighters fled the site. And, miraculously I escaped too. But regrettably my three compatriots Finn, Banny and Bob were captured by the enemy. Savagely the remorseless force barbarically shot them down in cold blood. In no time the vicious troops were hunting for me. In a desperate predicament I was on the run. Opportunely it was getting dark after sunset. And there was no moonlight. The situation forced the adversary to temporarily cancel the pursuit.

The following day I had scurried away for twenty kilometers in a bushy area when the defense forces chopper spotted me. Relentlessly the helicopter bombed twice in an attempt to kill me. Covered in the blown up dust I dogged and cheated death by a whisker. By then I disastrously ran out of ideas. The only safe option was to dive into a nearby burrow. Was it unassailable? This was a possible home to dangerous snakes, spiders or scorpions.

Meanwhile the copter repeatedly circled the sky. For almost forty minutes the environment was frightening. Though the pilot was extremely determined as he hovered overhead, all was in vain. In chilling fear, I felt awfully vulnerable. I dreaded the foot soldiers who walked and searched in the bushes. They posed great danger. Well aware of the hazardous quandaries I never coughed.

Suddenly a pronounced fidgeting developed inside the tunnel. What was it then? Was there a big snake close to me? I didn't know. Doubtlessly I was sharing the lair with a living creature. Despite the fact that it was scary I didn't move as there was a possibility of being annihilated by the killers.

Gradually the fierce chopper left. Was it a ploy? I didn't know then. Incredibly the airspace became quiet. But it was still dismally hair-raising.

By then the creature or creatures in the warren were restless. Gosh! What a harrowing experience that was. Confounded I quivered in an alarming state. Fainthearted I was afraid to die

Chilled to the marrow by fear I crouched close to the mouth hole, nervously peeping outside with one eye. Unexpectedly a critter forcefully blew warm air into my feet. Oh – o! Hell! That was scaring and life-threatening indeed. Agitated I whimpered in a low voice whilst trembling. Subjected to the dicey circumstance I blazed out of the hole. Incredibly two warthog piglets dashed out of the tunnel then sped off into the adjacent forest. In utter puzzlement I was terror-stricken for some moments. Then I gathered my bravery to move on. I had to hastily cross the border which separated Rhodesia and Mozambique. And within an hour I had cautiously sneaked into my destined territory of Mozambique in 1977.

CHAPTER 2

My former classmate, Cox, gave me a vague direction of the guerrilla bases in Manica province in Mozambique. I presumed that it was easy to locate them.

Nonetheless, bewilderment entangled me after arriving in that country. I didn't know where to go. Aimlessly I roamed eastwards into the heart of the province. From 6 a.m. to noon all I saw were animal droppings and their trails. The forest ecosystem was frightful. It was wooded too. Extreme silence punctuated the surroundings. And there was no human settlement. Unpredictably I saw big paw marks on a dusty ground. I wondered at the bizarre animal. Somehow I recollected an explanation from our former biology teacher who said lions had big paws. That triggered a bone-chilling panic in me. Perturbed I lost my courage.

As I walked into the tall dry grass unexpectedly two animals burst wildly from my left side. Dammit, one of them was heading towards me. At once I thought that was a lion which was coming to attack me. Never before had I screamed loudly in distress as I did. In utter horror and confusion, I tried to run away for safety. But I disgracefully fell down. As I rose up I saw the animal which had already made a u-turn. It was a large, hornless, female impala which was running away. Nervousness overwhelmed me. Then I sighed to release the tension.

Strangely a man in his early forties emerged from the bushes. Helpless and flabbergasted I stared at him. However, his welcoming face quickly eased my tautness. He was carrying a homemade gun (muguguda in Manyika language). The weapon was used for fighting enemies or for hunting purposes. He introduced himself as a hunter. And amicably we communicated very well.

In an inquisitive way I asked him if he knew Rhodesian African freedom fighters base camps in his country. Freely he gave me fruitful information. He pointed at the direction where a current establishment was. However, he lugubriously narrated how the former base was bombarded by enemy jets which resulted in the massacre of more than a hundred guerrillas and refugees. The brutal incident had happened about four months earlier. The new base was located in a valley about thirty miles away. Then he suggested that I had to use a circuitous route to avoid dangerous wild animals. I took heed of his recommendation before he left.

Rejuvenated, I briskly proceeded on my way towards the destination. I fell into an aardvark which was covered by dry grass. Although my left foot angle sprained, I limped on. Stench air filled the circumambient. A black object lay on my right side about fifteen meters on an open landscape. Curiously I went closer to see it. Oh gosh! It was a decomposing half eaten carcass of a kudu bull. Swarms of different flies congregated on it. It appeared to had been a week when the herbivore was killed. Flustered I cursorily left the scene as it seemed perilous.

CHAPTER 3

Late in the afternoon I was close to my highly desired dream destination. I couldn't wait to meet my beloved heroic strugglers.

From the top of the valley I saw some scattered, mud, grass thatched huts. The settlement appeared to had been densely populated.

The scotching heat did not spare me either. Sweat oozed from my body and soaked my clothes. As well hunger and thirst had made me weak. The roasted locusts and cicadas I had eaten on the way had not satisfied me. Desperately I needed some food to eat. Extreme pain from my cricked left foot angle was intolerable indeed. Slowly I wobbled as I descended the slope. Bubbling enthusiasm also propelled in me. Like a dream I entered the camp in a zealous mood singing the following revolutionary song:

English	Shona
Comrade! Comrade!	Gamba! Gamba!
Be resilient!	Rambai makashinga
Be resilient! x 2	Rambai makashinga! x 2

I jovially repeated the song on many occasions till I
met my hosts.

CHAPTER 4

Two soldiers on guard came forth to meet me. Affably and gaily I boldly moved towards them. Then, I opened my arms. to hug my beloved comrades. When the first guy was about two meters from me he panicked and jolted and retreated after scrutinizing my face. Vehemently he loudly screamed: "Oh devil! Jojo! Jojo! The deadly Boer spy has come again to wipe us out! Why? Why, on earth?"

Astounded and confused I stood still then stared at him. Like a nightmare I didn't figure out my circumstance. The other military man hastily came closer to me with a skeptical telling observation. Repeatedly he cautiously examined my face too. In no time he vociferously yelled: "Wow! Wow! It's incredible! I can't believe my eyes! This is Jojo, the betrayer! The sell-out! The traitor! Oh the damn killer is back here to get some information on our location and our population so that he could give the details to our enemy. Hell! Doubtlessly, we are in trouble again! Oh gosh! Oh gosh!" he then shook his head in fierce anger.

Defensively and fearlessly I rejected their allegations when I audibly and articulately said:

"I am not Jojo! I'm Ziff!" In anguish I repeated my name on five occasions. "I am Ziff! I am Ziff! I am Ziff! I am Ziff! I am Ziff!"

But the two soldiers never believed me. They stubbornly kept on saying: "Jojo! Jojo! The devil is here!"

CHAPTER 5

Wreathed in a harsh-regrettable scenario tears dripped down my cheeks. A dreadful ugly twist of events had engulfed my ambition. My survival was also hanging in the air. It appeared bleak. In extreme puzzlement I sweated in horror whilst utter hopelessness and nervousness devastated me.

As a result of the triggered alarm by the two fighters, anxiety among the camp dwellers fermented. Astonishingly an uncontrolled angry crowd converged on the site. The fighters hurriedly narrated their biased accusation on me. And, the mob became wild and agitated.

In a chaotic haphazard frenzy, the throng swarmed on me. I got into an intense vicious attack. Several punches were landed on my face. In severe pain I nose bled. I cannot recollect how I fell onto the dusty ground. The assailants angrily kicked my body and one chap spate my face. And, among the offending utterances the nasty crowd vented after pausing were: "You will regret today!"

"Damn traitor!"

"Your time on earth is numbered!"

"Notorious backstabber!"

"Savage betrayer!"

"Brutal bloke!"

"You won't send the spied information to our enemy because you are dying today!"

Suddenly an ugly, fierce military man burst onto the spot. He wore a commanding face. Immediately he shouted to everybody to stop the assault on me. They all obeyed his order. Whilst panting, he said: "Let's not kill the defector now. We need to investigate some strategic information he supplied to our adversary. As well, I need to verify if he is the culprit". One of the soldiers loudly responded: Fine commander Baga!

The curious military supremo instructed his subordinates to raise me on my feet. They quickly did it and I stood upright. Then the boss thorough inspected my battered pathetic face which was soaked by tears, blood and mucus. Vehemently his face dismally changed. What had he seen? I pondered.

Exasperated he shook his head. Burning with rage he pointed his right hand finger at my forehead and angrily said, "Dang! You are definitely the renegade and doubtlessly the most wanted for treason! Why did you leave our previous base camp to join our enemy, the Rhodesians? After that you came back in the archenemy jets which bombed us. You should be ashamed of your bloodletting diabolic activity! Man! You are responsible for the deaths of more than a hundred lives. Why in the hell did you do that?" The commander ferociously shouted. And, his followers stubbornly booed me. Meekly I said, "I don't know the allegations comrade! I'm Ziff! And not Jojo!"

The infuriated commander became restless when he said, "Shut up! Don't fool us!" We are ready to annihilate you! Okay!" I didn't talk anymore.

CHAPTER 6

The inflamed boss forcefully grabbed my shirt's collar. He vigorously raised my body slightly above the ground. Whilst I partially dangled in the air my windpipe was being choked. It became a critical struggle to breathe. Yet the big man had overpowered me. Was this my peril? I thought. Due to the lack of oxygen I was compelled to vomit directly on his face. Hey! This did not go well with him. He loathed the locust and cicada partially consumed food. Immediately in an atrocious manner he bashed me on the terra firma. In severe excruciating agony I became semiconscious whilst lying flat on the ground.

Meanwhile his stooges were celebrating as they presumed that I was dying. Then commander Baga picked me up. Completely weak I sat down and panted. However, slowly I gained my strength. Somehow I meekly spoke to my assailant. "Comrade --- are you determined to --- kill me? Why? I --- am --- really innocent." My words ignited his anger. He got terribly annoyed.

"Don't ever mention the word "comrade" to me! Never! Never address me in that status. You are not one of us! You are a disgraceful spy! A notorious deserter! Why? Why Jojo?" I needed to prove my innocence. "Absolutely --- I --- am --- one of your comrades!" I modestly said.

"Daggone! No! No! No! No! No! Man! Don't continue to spark my temper! This makes me to behave in an unrestrained manner. Hey! Don't play with me! Please don't! Your lying hours are limited. There is no doubt about this!", the military honcho fumed. His aids clapped hands in full support of his stance. The disgruntled, unruly mob chanted the following words, "We want to witness his death now! He should be buried today! More than a hundred of our comrades perished in his bloody hands! And there is no sympathy on the backstabber!"

A middle aged guy came forth and rudely jeered at me before he uttered the following words: "You are a devil! Today you won't escape any longer! We have precisely calculated your demise. And, we won't fail!" The wrathful man then went back to join the group.

CHAPTER 7

The military Chief gawked at me. He appeared to be antsy. Then he frowned his face before he spoke to me, "We have reached the time for your execution. Although it's almost sunset I need you to quickly dig your grave!" In spite that I looked frail, meek and submissive his barbaric determination to effect his results were paramount.

Promptly he ordered one of his soldiers to go and collect a pick, a shovel and a sjambok from the camp's storeroom. The junior darted to the depository. Within fifteen minutes he returned with the items.

The commandant instructed me to carry the pick and the shovel on my shoulders. I obeyed. The honcho got the battering ram in his right hand. Callously his face turned wild with anger.

Agonizing in excruciating pain I quivered. Thanatophobia shattered my courage. Hopelessly I didn't foresee my survival because I was surrounded by a fierce, hostile gang. It became totally unthinkable to escape.

The brute remorseless boss chose a man to lead me to the graveyard. I compliantly followed behind the assigned chap. All along the military supremo whipped my spinal area. Inconceivably I suffered from piercing sharp pain. I sighed dejectedly and whimpered then murmured repenting words whilst the pitiless horde energetically celebrated.

On arrival at the final resting place Baga enthusiastically pegged the size of my grave very close to two dug ones. The sun had already set and at gunpoint I was forced to dig my own grave. Due to exhaustion I failed to meet the required performance. And, the vicious army leader repeatedly flogged me hardheartedly. Blood oozed from some areas of my body. Drained and bone-tired I completed the undertaking. It was extremely dark at night. The frustrated commander said it was impossible to terminate my life as the majority of the residents had not turned up. The camp dwellers had to witness my capital punishment. He then scheduled the activity to dawn the following day. Emphatically he told the restless anticipating rabble to inform everybody to be punctual for the occasion. I shuddered with horror as I listened to the regrettable arrangement.

In a distraught way Baga ordered two battlers to take me to the camp's prison for the night. The hateful, arrogant guys tied up my hands using an old rope. In a violent move they kicked me all the way till I got into the grass thatched makeshift confinement. The assault was unendurable. After they had forcefully pushed me into the penal institution one of them locked the door.

CHAPTER 8

Hunched on a cold, pitch black prison I was downhearted at my plight. My mind recapitulated on the ferocious life-threatening ordeals I had encountered. Involuntarily tears trickled down my cheeks. Waving my hands up and down in the air in absolute anguish I poured my heart out when I questioned myself: "Why? Why, is this the end of my life? Why ---? Why ---? Why -------?"

I presumed that I was all by myself. But that wasn't it. From an inky corner of the cell came forth two men. We talked in low voices. And, the chaps narrated how they were sentenced to death by Baga. Subsequently they were forced to dig their graves. I then recollected the two excavated graves which were adjacent mine. Sadly, we were destined to be executed together the following day. Their hands were also tied by old ropes. Both men were in their mid-thirties. Then they introduced themselves as Bev and Zac. The latter relentlessly coughed.

We sank into despondency when we discussed about our bleak, ultimate deaths. The duo was completely dejected and hopeless.

Wholeheartedly I asked the guys if they had any strategic plans for our survival. They said they had no idea at hand. Cautiously I suggested a skeleton approach to escape from the prison through the roof. The area of the makeshift calaboose seemed weak.

The pair was somewhat very skeptical about the daring adventure. It was extremely afraid of being shot dead on the spot if we were caught in the act. Courageously I argued that it was a do or die risk because we were to be put to death in a few hours' time anyway.

After digesting the complicity of the issue the fellows hesitantly agreed. Using my teeth, I tactfully loosened Bev's rope in less than an hour. Reciprocally he undid Zac's and mine in a reasonable time. My nose seeped blood and Bev sympathetically gave me his blue T-shirt to wipe that off. I was touched by his companionship.

The correctional officers' shack was about forty meters from our cell. And, till about midnight the armed men spoke excitedly and loudly between themselves. It seemed highly likely that they were boozing. Then after a while the wardens were quiet. We assumed that they were drunk and had gone asleep.

We felt it was ideal to break free from the confinement. After a thorough assessment I opted to reach the roof of the institution. But I was very short to reach the target unless my cronies had to lift me up. They willingly did that. I then technically maneuvered and made our good exit.

We all agreed that when we broke out we were to head eastwards. The strategy was approved because Rhodesia is located west of Mozambique and if the commander dared to track us the following day we were to be captured on that direction. Therefore, our idea of heading the opposite direction was wise.

My colleagues suggested that I was to be the first to getaway. I concurred. They lifted me up and I intrepidly and cautiously sneaked out. When I had landed on the outside surface in the caliginous night, I waited for my associates. Auspiciously they safely came out too. Unwittingly Zac coughed ad infinitum. The noise awakened the law enforcement agencies.

The wardens' door was abruptly opened. Oh-o! At once we realized that we were inordinately vulnerable. Simultaneously we all dashed off in different directions into the gloomy night. Savagely the correctional officers randomly sprayed bullets towards us. Blessedly none of us was shot. The soldiers also wildly pursued us. Miraculously we managed to run away. It was dreadful and scary. Throughout the night I walked almost forty kilometers eastwards. At dawn I was wearied out. Then I looked for shelter. I found one below a shady tree. The disturbing issue was the seeping of the blood from my forehead. I had sustained a small wound during the life-threatening ordeal. There was no cloth to wipe off the gore. Alternatively, the broad leaves from a plant in an adjacent bush seemed to had been an option. Then I went into the shrubs and effectively used the leaves for the purpose.

CHAPTER 9

From a distance of about one hundred meters away I saw two men heading towards the east. Great devastation shuddered me. Were they Baga's forces hunting for me? I frantically wondered. In fright and restlessness, I lowered my whole body in the leafy foliage to avoid detection.

Critically I analyzed the individuals. One of them wore a blue T-shirt which resembled Bev's. And, another one had a khaki pair of trousers. Doubtlessly that was what Zac was putting on. I was totally convinced that the folks were my former inmates.

Jovially I burst out of the hideout bushes then ran to meet the chaps. On seeing me the men were panic-stricken and petrified by my feverish and sudden appearance. They yelled aloud as they nervously moved forward and backward in total confusion. Sadly, they had not recognized me.

However, with my repeated calls that "I am Ziff! I am Ziff! Guys! Don't be afraid!" Both persons stopped and listened properly. I shouted again and again. And, it appeared that they had recognized who I was. Wearing long troubled faces they came forth panting.

Full of excitement we amicably hugged each other. And, overwhelmed by emotions and regret we all recollected that by then we would had been executed and buried by Baga and his forces at the base camp. It was like a nightmare to be alive. Remarkably my counterparts showered lots of praises on my life saving strategy to escape. Noteworthy our bondage firmly cemented.

CHAPTER 10

We strode for about four kilometers west towards Rhodesia. The rich savannah vegetation had numerous wild fruit trees. Suddenly we were spoiled for choice. Our favorites were the snot apples and the monkey oranges. Happily, we ate the best we desired. Our hunger was no more. And we quenched our thirst from clean, fresh water in a large stream.

Leading our way was Bev. He noticed a big game dung. After a rough assessment we didn't establish the animal which had the excrement. Then we steadily continued on our journey. The grass was exceedingly tall and very dry. And, fairly tall trees dominated the landscape. We were then unable to see properly anything more than ten meters.

Head on, we inadvertently faced a dangerous confrontation. We had approached a sleeping rhinoceros and its calf. Hey! We winced aghast at the imminent danger. Demented we screamed aloud in absolute confusion as we retreated for about twenty meters.

The agitated and bewildered animal stopped and appeared as if she was ready to fight us. The beast growled and trumpeted angrily whilst her nurseling restlessly walked to and fro below her mother.

In an inflamed temper the monster shook its head and the long, sharp lethal horn signified ugly consequences for us. Befuddled we felt vulnerable. I quickly suggested an urgent idea of climbing a nearby tree for safety. My companions immediately agreed.

In a few moments we identified an ideal tree. Bev initiated to climb it followed by Zac and I was last. Bev's and Zac's branches were about nine meters above the ground and mine was close to seven. And, all our branches did not have any further provisions for ascending.

Unbelievably the impatient animal's suckling dashed towards us. We were extremely startled at why it decided to do that. In a berserk move the mother furiously came to attack us. Savagely it tried to push the tree down. By then her offspring was by her side. Then after a while the embittered monster led her calf away.

My ill-conceived suggestion to alight from the tree and continue on our journey was turned down by my cronies. They insisted that they were still puzzled by the unpleasant situation we had undergone. And, we remained clung to our branches.

Zac coughed interminably. The noise seemed to had attracted something else around the western side where we were supposed to go.

"Guys! Guys! I have seen two peeping ears." Bev exclaimed.

"What is it?" Zack queried.

"I didn't figure them out!" Bev replied.

"Why, Bev?" I questioned.

"Because the objects seem to have hidden in the tall grass!" Bev explained.

"Carefully check again, Bev!" Zac urged.

"Okay! Let me try again!" Bev responded.

Once more Zac coughed continuously.

"Oh hell! We are in trouble! We are in trouble!" Bev shouted out loudly.

"What is it, Bev?" I asked.

Bev appeared to be extremely agitated. His composure was completely rattled. He had noticed something.

"A lioness! Oh-o! A lioness! I --- have --- seen its --- ears protruding through --- the grass!" Bev blurted out.

The wave of uncertainty made us all to tremble with cold fear.

"Are you sure, Bev?" I courageously asked.

"Oh yes! Look at the gap between those bushes!" Bev pointed at the spot.

As we looked the varmint raised its dreadful head as it yawned.

"However, don't worry about that, folks! My father said lions do not climb trees like leopards. We are safe!" Bev gave us some confidence.

"Bev, don't fool us! That was wishful thinking from your dad." Zac disputed the notion.

In an alarming disappointment the lioness and its cubs came into our view. She majestically walked to us. Oh gosh! We quivered and frantically got dumbfounded.

Bev suggested that we had to make deafening noises to scare away the varmint. Intensely we repeatedly did that to no avail. Full of determination the brute came beneath us. Unbelievably it focused its eyes on me because I was at the lowest point. Its seemingly hungry cubs screamed and moved about in distress. Extreme bafflement gripped me.

To our bewilderment a massive frightful lion and a lioness came to reinforce the hunt. The might monster growled savagely as it looked at us. It appeared to be hungry too. We almost melted in alarm.

Meanwhile the lactating lioness started to climb the tree towards us. In a breathless state I was overwhelmed by horror, and involuntarily my tears were dripping down my cheeks.

"Dammit! Is the troublesome animal going to devour me today?" I hollered. My tormented bosom friends had no idea at all. Bev commanded us to hastily break the dry branches from the tree then forcefully bash the rogue animal's head. We did that. To our great surprise it showed immense determination when it came up slowly. In fact, the mischief animal became very aggressive and stubborn.

It was by then three meters away from me. Its left hind leg broke a twig where it had a firm grip. To our delight it fell down to the ground. I breathed a sigh of relief. In no time it gathered its strength and came up once more to its former position.

"It has --- come closer --- to me again!" I yelled.

"Absolutely we should defeat it! Why not?" Zac encouraged us.

As we severely struck its head, it roared bitterly and its stench breath filled my whole face. It looked very determined to grab me. Hey! I was hopeless when I looked at its devilish, wrinkled face and the sharp canine teeth as the vicious beast had gravely terrorized me. Would I survive? I nervously questioned myself.

Bev was by then struggling to break a fresh tree branch which was adjacent to him. But sadly the branch where he grasped broke off.

Dumbstruck and in a regrettable disbelief our dear brother Bev fell nine meters down onto the hungry lions' mouths. In a few moments the vicious starving man-eaters grabbed and tore his body into pieces as they violently fought among themselves to rip up his flesh. Even the whelps feasted on him, whilst the lioness disappeared with his head into the eastern bushes. It was a diabolic act. That's how Bev met his fate. Under intense fear we were dazed and garbled. Loudly I cried out:

"Oh-o-o-o! Oh-o-o-o! Oh-o-o-o! Oh-o-o-o! E-e-e- e-e- e! Why--- why ----? A-a-a-a-a-a! We--- miss---you---dear--- Bev---its---pathetic how---you---have---been killed--- and---eaten!" In severe panic Zac sobbed and some of his words were: "Shame ---! Shame---! What--- a sad--- tragic--- event! That's---an---incredible---loss to---me! Hey---! Hey---! A-a-a-a-a-a!"

The poem below is my heartfelt tribute to my former selfless and dedicated companion. Bev.

A Noble Sacrifice

Though you are gone,

To a world unknown,

We stood side by side,

Our vision being our guide,

Equipped by our desire to win

Bonded together as kith and kin,

You displayed an unfathomed love for me,

A noble sacrifice to die for me,

Bev, I am proud of your stand,

Selfless, till to the end,

What price should I pay,

To offset your terminal dismay?

Your departure left us unease;

And, may your soul rest in peace.

CHAPTER 11

Meanwhile the lion pride assembled and slept blithely beneath our tree once more. Our hearts disoriented. It was leaking its mouths after gobbling Bev's body. The rogue lioness lay flat in the dry, tall grass suckling her yearlings. It was highly likely that the pride was digesting a favorable meal it had eaten.

Though in severe distress Zac craved for a cigarette to smoke. He was not sure if he had any. Alas! He found four in his pair of trousers pockets. There was a lighter too. I was quick to say: "light them up and throw them burning onto the surrounding dry grass enclosing the hostile deadly creatures which were snoring." Urgently he did that.

Blown by the ruthless, strong wind the already blazing fire suddenly propelled and engulfed the brutes.

The belligerent's mane caught fire as it escaped, followed by its female mate. It was a horrendous scene as they all got totally confused. She tried to get away but failed. Consequently, it was wreathed in flames and perished with its cubs.

It was late in the afternoon when we were profoundly afraid to alight from the tree. The area was hazardous indeed. We agreed to spend the whole night holding tightly onto our branches like baboons.

Then at daybreak we clearly saw the burnt lioness and its cubs' carcasses in the ashes. There was no more fire. Moments later we witnessed the arrival of uninvited visitors. From the sky, above us a few tens of vultures descended. The birds majestically danced as they converged to feast on the roasted meat. The scavenging birds cunningly competed to tear open their feast as they wishfully desired.

Two jackals burst onto the site and rushed to chase their rivalry birds away. The duo promptly took their turn to munch the available remains. As if it was not enough, in about half an hour four hyenas also surfaced. The hyena family seemed to have been delayed to claim their share of the plunder. The vultures gave way to the bigger scavengers. The late comers went straight to rip open the lioness carcass. And, they did not hesitate to break the bones and chew them. The yearlings' left overs were not spared either by these greedy beasts. However, all the predators respected each other at different locations. At nightfall the birds took flight leaving behind their competitors searching on whatever was left on the ground.

During the critical time when we needed solidarity to focus our minds ahead in our mission to bolt for freedom, Zac sparked a prickly argument throughout the dark night.

The death of Bev shattered his courage. He completely lost hope in our expedition as he decided to make a u-turn so that we were to go and surrender to commander Baga. And, ultimately we were to be executed. Then he insisted that it was best to die in human hands then get buried than to be devoured by savage animals. I vehemently opposed his chicken-hearted move. My focus was to soldier on and, to be prepared to face whatever challenges which lay ahead of us.

CHAPTER 12

However, just before dawn Zac accepted my proposal to continue on our risky adventure. As we alighted from the tree we spotted a lone jackal which was looking for some leftover meat. I scared it away. And, before we moved off I suggested that each one of us had to be well equipped with a two-meter wooden rod to fight off the lions in the case the animals came forth to attack us. Zac was very pleased by the idea. We then looked around the bushes and selected excellent rods which we carried on our shoulders, ready to fight any attackers.

After walking on the burnt grass area for about four kilometers we entered into the tall grass and a savannah landscape. Accidentally we bumped onto three sleepy game. The animals abruptly panicked and jumped away in absolute confusion. It was alarming and horrific. We screamed in loud shouts. And, both of us dismally fell on the ground. Then we ran in one direction for safety. In puzzlement we threw away our rods. It was when we were about one hundred meters from the animals that we turned to see exactly the type of beasts these were. Gosh! They were harmless kudu cows. We failed to believe why we had no courage to confront any attacker. How about if these were lions?

We got into a peculiar phase. Zac was troubled by a flaming feeling. It seemed uncertainty rocked him. I didn't understand his odd attitude. In fury he showered nasty, offensive words to me. He accused me of being adventurous for nothing. I kept quiet. However, we proceeded on our mission.

The sky was covered by dark clouds late in the afternoon. Thereafter there was a tempest rainstorm which severely soaked us. In frightful lightning it became risky to walk on barefoot in the water. Ultimately we sort shelter below our shady tree.

At nightfall we climbed the tree for safety. And, we used our shirts to tie ourselves to the branches because we were afraid to fall down when we got asleep during the night.

The following morning, we got enlivened by viewing the breath-taking scenic western mountains. From our imagination we presumed the range stood on the border between Rhodesia and Mozambique, and we could hardly wait to get there.

CHAPTER 13

Determined we strode for almost seven kilometers before we arrived at a flooded riverbank. With acute prudence we assessed whether it was possible to cross it. The river was about nine meters wide and close to a meter deep. Zac boasted of his past expertise at crossing big and violent, flooded rivers. Convinced I banked on him as my performance was basically on a swimming pool level.

Zac identified an ideal portion of the river for our safe crossing. He firmly held my hand. Then energetically and skillfully he made us to cross it. Triumphantly we hugged each other after our success.

But our journey was bedeviled by incessant heavy rains. However, we managed to easily cross two other swollen risk- taking rivers. And, Zac daringly proved his masterly. By then after fifteen kilometers we were very delighted to see cow dung on several locations. However, we didn't see the animals and the herdsman. Then we got zealous to see a human settlement as we desperately needed food and the warm accommodation. But we didn't guess what lay ahead of us.

Only after four kilometers did we bump onto a flooded river again. It really didn't seem to be a major challenge because it looked smaller than all the rivers we had successfully gone over. But uniquely this one had muddy banks and thick reeds. And, as well it had a fast flowing current. Yet Zac did not dare to analyze any possible dangers. Though I lacked experience I suggested to him to properly examine the river. He utterly snubbed my admonitions. Nevertheless, I strongly relied on him. With dire vigilance we started to wade in the river. Zac tightly grasped my hand. Our steps were precise and well calculated.

Valiantly we had covered about five meters in the strong and fast-moving body of water when we realized that there was an awful slippery rock. Zac intensely became troubled.

Suddenly it became very unbearable for us. We got confused on whether to continue or to retreat. Somehow he loosened his tightness on my hand. Then I was on my own. I underwent a hair-raising severe torment. I hardly had any idea of how to overcome the imminent danger. It also appeared to be disastrous on him.

My companion was in front of me. Unprecedentedly he was hurled by a savage flush flood like a piece of paper. Quivering at the midst of the violent torrent I shouted loudly: "Zac! Zac! Swim! Come on friend! Swim! Man!" Bravely he strenuously struggled to swim but due to the prevailing hostile force he turned out to be losing the torrent. And, sadly he gave up.

The last glance I had of him was when he was being tossed by the deluge. What a horrid traumatic experience that was. I still had complete confidence that Zac was going to successfully swim to the bank of the river. However, did he make it?

CHAPTER 14

Befuddled I quavered at the middle of the powerful tide. To make matters worse my audacity was being shuttered. And, I was severely haunted by the Thanatophobia. In no time my feet were being lifted up. What would I do then?

Intensely the rush swept me down into the depth of the water. Gosh! I felt that I was going to perish. Arduously I daringly swam heading downstream and I managed to bring my head above the water. Unwittingly I was being drifted downstream. It was a do or die situation.

Whilst battling I noticed some dry logs, floating alongside me. In a haste I grasped a big one and then quickly went on top of it. Totally determined I steered it towards a protruding rock further down. It was extremely hard to sway it to my desired point. That was unbelievable. When I finally touched the rock I hurriedly climbed it.

For a while I panted and rested on top of a two-meter boulder. A terrifying huge pool surrounded me. I failed to figure out my next move. Then subsequently I thought of something.

The buoyant shriveled wooden chunks and branches which drifted close to me had some potential to make a nest around the rock. My circumambient atmosphere posed great danger. Bit by bit I assembled some material which came close to where I was, till I built something that looked like a hammercop nest.

Pouring heavy rains upstream caused the river to swell. The bottom part of my poorly built makeshift roost was by then sitting in the water. It was shaking badly too. This was an unacceptable development which bedeviled my survivorship. Where would I go then from here? I wondered. That was about mid-morning.

From my west came a cunning man-eater and seemingly hungry crocodile. Its ugly dreadful looking face shook my heart to melt with fear. Yet, the fierce reptile was dauntlessly coming forth. It was capable of destroying my clumsy dwelling and devour me. Unfortunately, I had lost my log during the trials to climb the boulder. But I had to fight the imminent enemy fearlessly. It was a life-threatening battle. And, would I win it?

My only weapon available was a two-meter sharp stick which I quickly picked from my collection. When the rogue reptile viciously encountered me without delay I thrust the sharp stick into its open mouth. It must had felt the severe pain as it unceremoniously swung back and dashed off. In disbelief I sighed. Due to the acute hunger I ate some of the semi-dry tree leaves which I took from the branches in my nest.

CHAPTER 15

For four days there was no rain. Consequently, the flood water receded. And, there was real hope to descend from the rock and cross the river. I hailed it as a potential opportunity. But I didn't survey the reeds and the mud along my path to reach the bank.

Prudently and tenaciously in the face of uncertainty I got into the muddy and reedy portions of the river. I carried a two-meter wooden rod. Sanguinely I covered about five meters on my way. Confidently I thought all was well. But, sadly I began to sink into the mud. From the initial knee high level in a short while I went down to about my chest level. And, the reeds were remarkably thick too. In an awful circumstance I found that I was in a precarious situation. My feet were completely stuck in the sticky mud and I failed to move out. Energetically I wouldn't make a u-turn or move out.

It was exceedingly cold too in the muck. The nights were insufferable. I mused and then sobbed.

Then from a distance of about five meters I noticed a systematic movement of the reeds. The arundo donax were shaking. Curiously I scrutinized the real cause. The creature's head was identical to a baby crocodile's. And, helpless and motionless I was likely to be vulnerable.

Oh my gosh! It was a big python. Dumbfounded and puzzled I cried my heart out in confusion. "Oh, why? Why should I be swallowed whole by a python? Am I dying today?" My noise frustrated it. Then it halted a bit. Nevertheless, its atrocious eyes were focused on me. And, stubbornly it did not give up. As well I made up my mind to fight my attacker valiantly to the end. Firmly in a staunch manner I held my rod in my hands. That was my only weapon to save me from an oncoming danger. Would I fortuitously defend myself anyway?

Indubitably the villain reptile moved resolutely to attack me. It was about three meters away. Though I was partially dazed by nervousness I recoupled my boldness and raised my rod in the air. Then without any hesitation I energetically bashed its head on numerous occasions when it was very close to me. As well I battered its eyes.

Unquestionably it had backed off from my decisive aggressive assaults. Its whole body movement was like locomotive coaches in motion when it dismally disappeared into the thick reeds. Unbelievably relieved I sighed.

CHAPTER 16

My ambient proved to be disastrous indeed. Desperately I needed an urgent rescue. I recollected the cow paths a few kilometers from the river. And, I suspected that there was a human settlement within the vicinity.

I yelled to the point of screaming. But there was no response. It was late in the afternoon and I was acutely scared to remain in the savage surroundings. And, of great danger was a violent rainstorm upriver. The chances of flooding were very likely. If I remained stuck in the mud the inundation was possibly going to swamp me. Then obviously I would lose my life.

Due to the intense emotions and apprehension I hollered for help once more. Repeatedly I shouted out, gasped and panted. After a while a man appeared along the riverbank. We spoke loudly for proper communication. He was very amicable and sympathetic at my ordeal. What a wonderful herdsman he was. He had lost his cow and had suspected the animal to have been killed by crocodiles in the river. That is why he was searching for the beast in the pools.

The stockman suggested that I remained calm as he was rushing to see his headman. And, he expected the village leader to help me. My mental tension cooled down.

As I waited the flash flood was swelling considerably. This was a result of the upstream downpour. Although the water level was still fairly low the fragile situation was crucial and unpredictable. And, the chilling fear of death hounded me too. Despite the fact that I didn't know the distance where the cattleman had gone my expectation for his return was fading. As well I was getting nervous by the minute.

Expeditiously a crew of four men arrived including the herdsman. It had a wheelbarrow, two buckets of clean water and a very long rope. In no time one guy threw the cord to me. After several attempts of failure, I grabbed the rope at last. Without wasting time, I tied it round my armpits. The four men easily pulled me out of the mess. Like a nightmare I was saved from the catastrophic tribulations. My tears inadvertently rolled down my face when I recapitulated my fate. And after a short while I regained my tenacity. Then I sincerely acknowledged the team's remarkable assistance.

The squad laid me in the wheelbarrow. Unfeigned it thorough washed me and my muddy clothes. By then my feet were very weak and I wouldn't stand or walk well. The guys were exceedingly helpful and pitying. Within one hour we were at headman Gara's residence.

What a polished man Mr. Gara was. His hearty cheerfulness and accommodating manner was second to none. He requested his wife to prepare some nourishing food for me. The roasted chicken was tasty and delicious indeed.

From nowhere I found that Mr. Gara was profoundly altering my whole course of life. He gave me lots of second hand clothes and shoes. I was extremely amazed at his exceptional hospitality.

In a detailed discussion with him I raised my grave concern about Zac's fate. Immediately he sent another group of five men to go and search for Zac's whereabouts along the riverbank. He recommended that I remained behind so that I was to rest. Absolutely I accepted his advice.

After three hours Zac's partially decomposed body was brought to the headman's forecourt in a wheelbarrow. The copse was picked further down from where I had survived the horrendous ordeal. Regrettably some vultures and jackals were already helping themselves on his flesh when the crew arrived. In shock and intense sorrow, I rolled on the dusty ground weeping miserably.

The headman and a few onlookers were emotionally moved. It was preposterous to imagine that he had passed on. And, severe low spirits choked me.

The whole village converged at headman Gara's house to pay its respect to my deceased compatriot. The traditional leader narrated a brief story about me. He earnestly highlighted how I was swept by the flash flood then miraculously survived on a solitary rock at the middle of a fierce pool of water.

Then in four hours we buried Zac's body beneath a snot apple tree. Overwhelmed by the trauma and devastation I privately mourned for his death in seven days.

CHAPTER 17

In an amazing gesticulation I was spoiled for choice on foods by Mr. Gara. He provided me with beef, chicken and fish as well as a wide variety of vegetables. In about a fortnight my health had rejuvenated drastically. The headman had a beautiful daughter named Olinda. She was of my marriage age. In a nutshell, she was fairly beautiful and well mannered. Her father always asked her to accompany me to various destinations around the community. Later on I perceived that he wanted me to marry her. But I had no intention to do that. However, I didn't show any negative attitude on the issue.

What would I do on the calculated, sensitive plot? I was seriously and tactfully cornered. Yet I desperately needed to remain in his custody. If I objected to his decision, I was likely going to be chucked away. I thought of an alternative approach. In no time I proposed love to Olinda. Doubtlessly she positively responded. To drag the time for our wedding to six months later was to provide me with enough period to assess the situation. Both Olinda and her parents accepted my schedule.

Whilst the family's expectations were high I suffered from a severe malaria attack. The big boss was dismally distressed at my ailing health. However, he knew some traditional medicines for the cure of the disease. Convincingly he prescribed the medication to me and I was left with no option to refuse the offer. And, as well he assigned Olinda to nurse me.

For almost a fortnight my condition turned out to be grave. Mr. Gara was disturbed. However, a week later I recovered miraculously well. By then the honcho was exhilarated at my condition. In his exceedingly joyous mood, he gave me some pocket money.

Eventually the traditional leader was preparing for my permanent stay in the community. He discouraged me from going back home to Rhodesia which was still under the colonial rule and heavy fighting between the insurgents and the government forces was in progress. And, among his fabricated scaring stories was the numerous deaths along the border due to the anti-personal mines. He warned me to avoid the calamitous adventure. I seriously took heed of his advice and agreed to stay on. But my vision was unfathomed.

Deplorably bad the neighborhood experienced a violent harmful cholera outbreak. The disease claimed the lives of many dwellers including Mr. Gara's younger brother. His family and the hamlet got awfully grieved.

This plunged us into a sorrowful time. And, unexpectedly I was infected with the disease too.

Oh hell! In a short time, I battled with an uncontrolled vomiting and diarrhea. My hope for survival was questionable. Mr. Gara asked his daughter to care for me. And although he advised me to take a lot of fluids my condition was worsening by the hour.

Somehow he remembered a dependable old friend who was in charge of a medical international organization based in Chimoio, the capital city of Manica province. He immediately suggested that we had to go to the institution. I agreed. Wholly unfeigned he took me in his old automobile to Chimoio. In spite that the road was rough we traveled for forty kilometers and arrived safely at our destination. Prudently Mr. Gara met his former mate, Ms. Marija, a Yugoslavian doctor. He persuaded the physician to urgently treat me. She earnestly accepted. In no time I was put into an intensive care unit. Under her exclusive supervision I was out of danger in two days. Like a dream I was recuperating steadily to the amusement of both Mr. Gara and Ms. Marija. Well contented that I was out of danger he made up his mind to return to his home. And, he left.

CHAPTER 18

After my recovery from the dangerous disease I relaxed on the lawn whilst enjoying the warmth of the sun outside the medical establishment. A boy of about fifteen years came forth from the west wing of the premise. He showed an inquisitive look at me. It was a critical assessment of my face. Then he nodded and looked puzzled

Brazenly he looked straight into my eyes as he stood about two meters from me. In a wild manner he pointed at my forehead using his right hand finger before he loudly shouted, "Hello Jojo! Jojo, the notorious escapee! The treacherous betrayer! Oh-o! Bastard! I have got you at last!"

Baffled and confounded I harshly replied him. "Don't accuse me on downright falsehoods! Who are you?"

Full of rage he said, "I was one of commander Baga's insurgents who found you guilty of treasonous and devilish activity when you masterminded the bombing of our former military base by our enemy, your bosom friends! In that attack more than one hundred innocent lives perished. Because of you! You are really aware of this! Are you not ashamed of this heartless undertaking? Why did you do that?"

Turbulently I felt completely irritated when I shouted at him saying, "Dammit! Get away from here! Damn liar! Don't call me Jojo! I am Ziff! Man!" After rebuking him he cowardly backed off. And, as he discourteously walked away, he loudly said, "We will fix you good. Sooner or later!"

Flabbergasted I stood still and absolutely startled. Nevertheless, I gathered some confidence and I sadly went into Ms. Marija's office. It took me about an hour to fully explain to her my comprehensive horrendous ordeal when commander Baga and his group tormented me. Initially her response was negative but when I sobbed and wept she was touched. Distressed she desired to know the truth on the matter. Without wasting time, she went to see the boy. On her return I was very pleased to hear her statement. She was convinced that the allegations leveled against me by commander Baga were fabricated and baseless. But of great concern was the possibility of the boy who was likely to go and inform the military supremo of my whereabouts. If that happened the military chief was highly likely to come and seize me for execution.

Ms. Marija precautionary decided to quickly hide me somewhere before making my final flee from the vicinity.

She resolved that I had to hide in her house's ceiling where coughing and fidgeting were not acceptable at all cost. I agreed and settled in the hideout. At all times she cautiously kept the ceiling gate closed.

At one occasion when Ms. Marija brought some food for me she requested for my academic qualifications. I clearly remembered them. She was very impressed at the distinctions on my science subjects, especially Biology and General Science.

A day later she wanted to know if I was interested in doing a medical degree at her former University in Yugoslavia. I said I was interested.

In three days she had secured a place and a scholarship for me to enter the University. Gladness overwhelmed me. I was amazed by the opening of a golden opportunity in my life. And cheerfully I was profoundly grateful for her exceptional help.

CHAPTER 19

Two days later at almost midnight, Ms. Marija's front door was barbarically banged. I saw everywhere in the house through a small opening. She was terribly offended as she shouted, "Who are you? Why are you damaging my door?"

The door was forcefully opened and six armed men savagely entered the house. Among them was commander Baga and the fifteen-year-old boy who had a nasty argument with me at the medical complex. All of them pointed their guns at Ms. Marija's face. Absolutely dumbfounded she quavered in mind-boggling fear.

Full of rage the man in charge spoke in a hoarse voice: "I am commander Baga! Where is Jojo, the conspirator? He is here!"

Petrified and scared Ms. Marija trembled as she answered, "I --- don't know --- the chap! I am --- alone --- in here!"

Fuming with fury the military chief said, "Stupid woman! Come on! Man! We need him! Where is he? Show us! Now! Now! He is a sell-out escapee!"

Ms. Marija nervously said, "Look --- for --- him --- elsewhere! He is not in here!"

Impatiently the fierce Baga ordered his subordinates to search everywhere in the house. And, the armed chaps vigorously overturned the beds and thoroughly looked in the wardrobes and behind every household effects. They dismally found nothing.

By then I was jittery and apprehensive. And, I had already wrapped myself in a blanket to falsely look like a rubbish heap.

The boss was panting. And he wore a long frustrated face. Suddenly he pointed his gun at Ms. Marija's face and said, "If you don't tell us where the traitor is, I will shoot you! Okay! Don't play with me!" The military supremo indignantly said. Ms. Marija knelt down pathetically and pleaded, "Kindly --- spare --- my --- life, please! I am innocent!" Exasperated and irritated the chief commanded his men to leave the room. Downhearted the group went into the dark night.

CHAPTER 20

Indubitably I was highly likely to have been killed by the brutal clique. The agonizing distressful event gripped me with horror. For two nights I failed to sleep.

In the meantime, the selfless Ms. Marija had successfully bought my airfare ticket and had also secured the plane booking. I was then scheduled to fly from Beira in Mozambique to Belgrade in Yugoslavia the following day at night.

She asked me to alight from the ceiling before dawn. Delighted I hastily prepared and we cautiously sneaked away from Chimoio to Beira before sunrise. After our arrival at the destination at about 9 o'clock in the morning she took me for breakfast in a local hotel.

It was an indelible occasion. As we sat relaxing in the lounge of the hotel I gave her my sincere gratitude for the immeasurable help and sacrifice she offered me. In an ecstatic mood she earnestly pledged to continue to assist me in times of my challenges.

As we were taking soft drinks early in the afternoon Ms. Marija received a telephone call from her office which had a sad message of Olinda's death from a cholera disease. I was dismally wretched to hear of her passing on. In agony I quietly sobbed and wiped away my tears in sorrow. Ms. Marija was grievously affected too. And, tactfully she consoled me. I explained to her that Olinda was Mr. Gara's daughter who nursed me when I suffered from the deadly cholera. Blameworthy conscience haunted me as I presumed that I infected her with the disease when she cared for me.

Then I took a piece of paper and a pen and then wrote a letter to Mr. Gara. Ms. Marija was to hand the letter to her employee who was to deliver it to Mr. Gara. The following is the content of the written message, "There are no words to describe my sadness at the passing on of Olinda, your daughter. She was truly a best friend anyone could have in his/her life. I was so lucky to have had a life with her. I deeply cherished the care she gave me and I'm sincerely thankful for the amazing memories I have of her. She will be so very missed by your family and me. I will forever keep in my heart and remember the life of an incredible human being."

It was time for me to board the plane. And, I bid farewell to the distinguished honorable lady, Ms. Marija. Sorrowfully, she gazed at me as I disappeared.

CHAPTER 21

On landing from the plane at Belgrade Nikola Tesla airport I was welcomed by two students from the University where I was destined to go. We went in a school car to my dream come true institution.

After a warm welcome from the school receptionist I was led by the students to my allocated dormitory where I was introduced to three roommates. Those who introduced me left.

My first unique problem was the language. The nation spoke a Serbo-Croatian, Bosnia Herzegovina language. The scholars didn't know English. Our relation in the room was tense and absurd. It appeared as if I had invaded the guys' territory. In fact, their body language spoke louder than words. A negative attitude prevailed in them. And, when I tried to speak to them they simply scoffed at me.

Yet their president Josip Broz Tito had offered the third world countries his unfailing love and brotherhood. He invited foreign students to study in his institutions. What an overindulgent leader he was. That was the reason why I didn't hesitate to go to his country.

After having exhausted every possible means to show my friendship with the tripartite pupils I then resorted to meet the head of the college. Although he understood English his modus operandi had little focus on the president's mandate. He didn't have a clear-cut decision to thwart my ill treatment from the fellow learners. However, he emphasized that I had to quickly learn their local language. I agreed. Then he gave me the full curriculum for the medical course.

When my roommates Zoran, Slavica and Vakasin went for meals in the dining hall I followed them. When they stopped walking I also stopped. It seemed they needed me to expose my ignorance. What an underrating and humiliating experience that was. And, the life in the dorm with the tutees was obnoxious.

They would deliberately mess the toilet and rudely command me to clean it. Partially smoked cigarettes, toothpicks and used papers were thrown on the floors and I was ordered to sweep the dirt away. They also didn't wash the utensils they used in our small kitchen. I was forced to clean them. Meekly I endured the traumatic inhuman treatment for almost five months. That negatively impacted on my academic performances too. I felt totally subdued. Where would I go then?

Opportunely in the sixth month I met a British born Yugoslavian student, Bogdan. His name in English means God given. We were in the same class and he was eloquent in English and Yugoslavian languages. He was a cheerful and a helpful guy. In no time we became close friends and I desperately leaned on him in a wide spectrum of issues.

Eventually he tactfully cultivated my interest in the much sort after local language. It improved immensely. As well I scored impressive pass rates in all my subjects.

Bogdan brazenly took me to the dormitory caretaker. He explained to the janitor my fundamental problems. Then he skillfully persuaded the warden to effect some accommodation transfers. So I was to vacate where I stayed and I had to join him. The custodian agreed, and he perfectly did the swapping undertaking. In a day everything was sorted out. It was extremely incredible. And, with confidence I mingled with fellow learners in a happy ambitious scholarly way.

There was a thrilling time for athletics in the college. My record of attainment in the activities at my previous high school was noteworthy. I enjoyed running. Voluntarily I joined the varsity team under Mr. Dragas, the sports master.

Because I was the only black chap in the educational institution, the man in charge underrated my capabilities. As well my former biased roommate, Zoran was among the competitors. Peculiarly my antagonist came close to me and spate my face, without any provocation. Then he went away. Gosh! What a disgusting evil act that was. Burning with anger I almost smacked him. I was choked by the fear of deportation from the country if I had sparked a retaliatory fight. But indignantly I moved to and from whilst sobbing. A few moments later the rogue joined us.

As the sports activities started off I was matched against seven best runners in the college for a hundred-meter race. With exceptional, strenuous high speed I outstandingly won the first position among them. Almost everyone on site was startled. It was beyond their expectation. Some inordinately excited students shouted loudly, "Ziff! Ziff! Ziff!" And Mr. Dragas was overwhelmed too. The physical education instructor came forth and hugged me tightly then shook me in disbelief. Zoran, who was close to him was troubled by fuming jealous.

In subsequent races I proved unequivocally good and I was a force to reckon when I won a second and a third position. The racial prejudice in the varsity was fading gradually. The name Ziff was by then highly esteemed in the corridors.

Most scholars loved soccer. The man in charge of the sport grouped us all into four teams.. Sensitive football (Nogomet, Serbo-Croatian language) rivalry circulated among the pupils. My choice was Nogomet Wamnnah or Football Champions in English. That was because Bogdan, my beloved friend was in the team. And, we earnestly played together in harmony. After a thorough assessment of my capability I chose to play at number ten position.

Fortuitously we were paired against the best team. There was cowardice fever which agitated my colleagues. They openly confessed that our squad was incompetent to defeat our opponent. After our intense training I didn't believe their assumption.

In a strained ambiance the game kicked off. After almost thirty minutes of play there was pandemonium when I deftly dribbled my adversaries then wormed my way into their gate with the ball. An explosive applause and uncontrolled cheering filled the late afternoon air. The echoes of "Ziff! Ziff! Ziff!" were incredible in the playground which was surrounded by buildings. As if it was not enough our teammate headed a corner ball into their net. The second score totally silenced our rival.

And, the successive two semesters witnessed our invincible performance in the varsity.

A calculated devilish agenda was crafted by a competitive team's footballer. When we had very little tackling to possess the ball, he deliberately crushed my left foot's angle bone. Hell! In excruciating pain, I rolled on the ground. I was in agony. And it was severely unbearable.

Urgently I was attended to by the First Aid crew. An ambulance was called and I was taken to a nearby hospital. Bogdan was on my side. Doctors carried an x-ray on the specific spot. They found my angle bone awfully cracked. And, straightaway the medical team wrapped a plaster cast around the injured portion.

CHAPTER 22

Lugubriously for four months I was hospitalized. Quite amazing The University Vice Chancellor irregularly brought various food staffs when he visited me on my hospital bed. I was overwhelmed by his boundless love.

But regrettably my inevitable absence from lecture attendances ruined my academic attainment. On the other hand, my unwavering bosom buddy, Bogdan, tirelessly came close to my bed with lectured notes. To a great extent that helped me out. I ran short of words to give him my utmost gratitude for his fabulous work. And when I was discharged from the medical institution, in a wheel chair, he pushed me into the lecture rooms. and any other locations. It was a challenging task for him.

Nevertheless, I battled like a wounded buffalo to overcome my imminent pitfalls. Rigorously and restlessly I studied without ceasing day and night. My lecturers were extraordinarily helpful in every way.

As a result, my academic results at the end of my medical degree were stunningly impressive. My bandage was removed. And, obviously my absence in my football team was a setback. The squad bounced back to ridiculous poor performances.

I was scheduled to leave Yugoslavia and a small farewell party for me was organized by the Vice Chancellor, Mr. Ranko, in his office. The invitees were Mr. Dragas, my stalwart lecturer Mr. Nikica and my soul mate, Bogdan. We feasted on satiating food.

Skeleton speeches came from the small gathering. Mr. Ranko said I was a diligent and a polished scholar. He also felt that it was an honor to had been part of the academy. Bubbling with exhilaration, Mr. Dragas noted on my inspiration and vigor in sports spirit which stirred and ignited the other athletes. The energetic convivial Mr. Nikica applauded on my resilience in learning and the propelling winning spirit. Then the inexhaustible, sprightliness friend, Bogdan, dramatized my fearless character when I discharged my duties. I was emotionally affected. And, modestly and wholeheartedly I expressed my profound gratitude to all my superiors for the immeasurable assistance they offered me.

In an ecstatic sentiment Mr. Ranko handed me my sought after medical degree certificate and a closed envelope in which was a cheque. What a dream come true that was, to be a physician. Triumphantly I floated on the air.

From the time I went to Yugoslavia I had always kept a cordial rapport with Ms. Marija who consistently paid for my upkeep. I had notified her of my schedule to leave the varsity after graduation. Without wasting time, she bought my flight ticket to return to Zimbabwe, my home country. My venerated companion, Bogdan, was awfully affected by my leaving his country. I was also heartbroken by our separation which was inevitable.

We left the airport in my hired taxi. Perturbed we hugged each other before I boarded the plane. Spontaneously my tears flowed down my cheeks. I was deeply touched. Then I ascended onto the plane's platform. Like a dream I left him downhearted and gaping.

CHAPTER 23

Boggled with high emotions and expectations I witnessed the hovering of our plane above the Salisbury Airport. I wouldn't wait to land on our independent state of Zimbabwe. It was like a nightmare.

Upon landing on the airport tarmac I saw THE ZIMBABWE INTERNATIONAL AIRPORT and the town's name HARARE. Instead of THE RHODESIA AIRPORT and Salisbury city. Wow! I dearly emulated the latest development. That was in 1982, almost three years after attaining the independence.

However, as I pushed the trolley loaded with my bags a friendly guy came forth to help me to shove my stuff. I agreed. He was considerably intelligent. Then he initiated a dialogue with me. I welcomed it. Avidly, I needed to know from him the news on the ground as I questioned him on the dream come true freedom.

In an honest and straightforward way, he said, "Brother, this is a contentious scenario."

"What do you mean?" I queried.

"Let me introduce myself." He said.

"Okay! Go ahead." I accepted.

"I am Tonderai! In English it means Remember!"

"I'm very pleased to know you Tonderai. And, I am Ziff!"
I responded.

"Now let me tell you the truth." He fearlessly talked.

"Go ahead, Tonderai!" I approved.

"Our government has done a tremendous effort in
education. Several schools have been built across the
nation, and a few Universities have been established.

Racial discrimination is being addressed and Africans
are buying upmarket houses where Europeans stayed
alone. However, not many of us are able to afford to
own the institutions.

Prices of basic commodities are sky-rocketing and the
government is gunning down the protesters a similar
heinous activity which was done by the colonialists.

And, corruption is fermenting. As well tribalism,
nepotism was taking a center stage. What did the
comrades fight for?"

I was awfully bored by his anti-government utterances. I
was by then very impatient when I said, "Get away,
devil! You scoundrel! An unrepentant sell-out! Damn,
imperialist agent! To hell with you! You should

appreciate what the freedom fighters have finally brought to the nation!" Infuriated I was filled with melancholy and despondency as I stood for seven minutes digesting the mystifying dialogue I had with the chap.

Tonderai was by then uneasy and before he rushed into the airport corridors he said, "Don't protect the looters! Guerrillas fought for nothing! Okay!" Then he darted away.

CHAPTER 24

Cognizant of not having a relative in the town I hired a taxi to take me to my rural home. On my way I put on my medical degree gown in a store's fitting room midway to my destination. It was almost noon when I arrived at my parent's doorstep. Both my mum and my younger brother, Joe, were in the house. Their voices were clearly distinguishable.

The moment I stepped into the abode their hearts nearly melted in panic. It seemed everyone's nerves were shattered. Beyond their expectations they were dumbfounded. If I had appeared to them during the dark night, they might had presumed that I was a ghost.

Nevertheless, they screamed incredulously and their utterances filled the room. Joyously they jumped back and forth. Repeatedly I commanded them to calm down, in vain. However, at last after almost twenty minutes they chilled out.

Down-to-earth we affably hugged each other. However, mum was still disturbed when she spoke, "My --- son! My --- son! My beloved --- son! Ziff!"

"My --- precious mum!" I humbly responded in a hysterical manner.

"Where --- were --- you --- all these --- years? Tell --- me!"

"Mom --- I had gone --- for the liberation --- of --- our --- country!" I cordially answered.

"Then --- what --- happened, Ziff?" she earnestly queried.

"I --- will --- tell you --- mum, when I have --- a convenient --- time!" I compassionately said.

"I mourned --- and --- grieved --- for you --- as I thought --- you were --- dead, Ziff! Oh-o-o! My --- son ---! I am exceedingly --- happy --- to see you --- alive!" she heavy heartedly said.

"Oh --- well --- mum! I'm --- back!" with confidence I acknowledged her.

"It's like --- an ephialtes!" Then she sighed.

"And what's this gown for, brother Ziff?" Joe inquisitively asked.

In a respectful way I explained, "It is a medical degree garment which is given to a learner after passing the standard. The recipient is called a general practitioner or a medical doctor."

"Wow! You are a doctor! I can't believe you!" Joe joyfully exclaimed.

"Yes, I am, brother!" I concurred.

"Congratulations! Congratulations, brother! What a major breakthrough in your life! Well done!" he wholeheartedly said.

Somehow mum seemed to had been fairly absent-minded during my dialogue with Joe. But she got that I was by then a doctor.

"Do you mean that you are a doctor, Ziff?" she seriously questioned.

"Yes mum! Exactly I'm!" I emphasized.

"E-e-e! Doctor Ziff! Hey! I'm proud of you! My --- son! I'm very glad! Well --- done! Well done! I can't believe you!" Overwrought she jubilantly moved back and forth.

"Thanks mum!" contentedly I welcomed her comments.

"How I wait to be treated by you, sonny!" she excitedly cracked a joke.

"I will help you mum." I reverently assured her.

"Ok my son! That was my long awaited dream. And, now it's fulfilled." She nodded in a cheerful spirit.

Something popped into my mind. Why was dad not among us? At once I asked, "Mum, where is dad? I'm yearning to see him!"

Engulfed in sadness she paused a bit before she talked. In a heart-broken frame of mind she said, "He --- died --- four years ago! I am still --- in low spirits --- up to now!"

"What did you say, mum?" I burst in disbelief and trauma as I queried her. "Dad --- is --- no --- more, Ziff!" dejectedly she murmured. Suddenly a flood of feelings of grief triggered in me. Severely bewildered I whimpered and shook my head in anguish.

"I wanted --- to --- tell dad of my --- medical success. As well --- I desired --- to show him my gown ---! Oh --- o-o! But --- he --- is --- never to be seen again!" mournfully I uttered unanswered issues as I moved to and fro in the room. Both mum and Joe cautiously cooled me down. "Brother Ziff, please accept what happened. Unbelievably our adventurous luminary beacon which navigated our lives, died. It's very sad indeed that he succumbed to the deadly malaria disease." Joe grievously said.

CHAPTER 25

Our vociferous noise alarmed the entire village. Unexpectedly people had milled around our house. They were full of aghast to know what was happening in our residence. Promptly the three of us hurried out of our dwelling to meet them.

Baffled at seeing me my former friends yelled without restraint then raised me on their shoulders happily and shouting, "Ziff! Ziff! Ziff! Welcome home, dear bosom friend!" My acknowledging words were completely overwhelmed by the uncontrolled pandemonium. Some women and girls reverberated their distinct words of praising me. My mom's tears of joy were dripping irresistibly down her face. The headman, Futa ordered everyone to stop the commotion. And, they all obeyed him. Merrily he came forth and embraced me in deep affection. In a whispering voice I summarized my adventurous journey. And, in both exultant and puzzlement he said to his audience that he was impressed to hear how I persevered through my calamities. In addition, he had a few words to notify his subjects. In a decisive move he urged them to contribute generously, assorted meat, fish and any other edible foodstuffs for my BIG WELCOME BACK the following weekend.

In elation he wholeheartedly and jubilantly shouted, "Doctor Ziff! Doctor Ziff! Welcome home! We are very proud of you!" Reciprocally his followers repeated his words as they all wildly cheered and congratulated me before they left the scene.

CHAPTER 26

By coincidence I got an opportunity to meet an amicable, helpful man who told me that his cousin had graduated as a physician in Romania a fortnight before me. And, on comparing the student's pass rates in almost every subject, I had scored far better than him. And, when the student went to see the deputy minister of health he was employed at once. He came from the top guy's province.

The following day I set of on a road map to seek employment in the capital city of Harare. Avidly, I headed to the Ministry of Health.

At about 10 a.m. I saw the deputy minister of the department. He was happy with the pass rate of my subjects. And, he was worried about the direful shortage of doctors in the country. We exchanged various thought-provoking jokes when he inquired about the life in Yugoslavia.

All along we had conversed in English. By then he requested to see my identity card. It bore my detailed information regarding the district and the province where I came from. After analyzing the information, he immediately showed a negative attitude towards me. His equivocal sentiment troubled me. Then he walked to an office further down the corridor. For almost twenty minutes he was busy in there.

Upon his return into his office he told me to go and see the Permanent Secretary in a specified bureau. Then I went into the office. Grudgingly, a cheerless, bearded, big man who was wearing a white suit knew all about my story. He asked me to fill in an application form. When I had finished he attached it to my duplicate degree certificate. His name was R.I.P. Godo.

Astonishingly he said the chances for employment were very slim. However, he said he was prepared to try and secure me a post. Somehow his body language spoke louder than words. It seemed as if he wanted something from me. I didn't know the concept. Having noted my ignorance of his secret demands without fear or shame he confidently raised his right hand palm then he spread out all his fingers. In a coercive way he stated that I had to do my assignment for him so that he was to reciprocally assist me. And, the money was simply to buy beer.

In that regard I asked him what the five fingers were worth. He said each finger represented ten United States dollars and therefore the five meant fifty dollars. I didn't have the money at all. Then he rudely suggested that I had to come back when I had the money. Wholly disappointed I moved out of his office.

CHAPTER 27

On my way from the Ministry of Health I arrived at a street intersection of Julius Nyerere Way and Samora Machel Avenue. A number of pedestrians were handing out money to a man who was seated in a wheelchair. Driven by passion I felt obliged to help him too.

When I had a closer look at the big guy I was emotionally flabbergasted. Who was this fellow? Wow! He was none other than Comrade Baga, the former camp commander at the liberation base in Mozambique. On affectionately greeting him, intently he doubtlessly recollected clearly who I was. Filled with remorse he was choked by his regrettable undertakings and he never spoke a word. He only shook his head in utter disbelief. Repentantly he floated in a troubled mind.

Determined I sparked a conversation with him, "Jojo! Jojo! The betrayer! The traitor! The sell-out!"

Wholly distressed he appeared demented by his previous activities. Then he cried out loudly which alarmed the street passers-by to converge around his wheelchair.

In no time he started to address the apprehensive crowd with a high pitched voice as if he was demon possessed, "My fellow citizens! I don't know how I can confess to this young man? I accused him as a betrayer, as a traitor and as a treacherous chap at a liberation camp which I commanded in Mozambique. My junior comrades and the refugees severely brutalized him. And, I sentenced him to death. I also commanded him to dig his own grave. Whilst he was in my prison he escaped during the night with two other condemned inmates.

After their disappearance I ordered my armed groups to pursue and kill them. But the forces failed to locate the escapees. Shamefully I met the real culprit, "Jojo", in one of the streets. The traitor confessed to me that he committed the heinous act. The young man standing by my side was innocent. He is also slightly different from the notorious evil doer." Then Comrade Baga pathetically whimpered. Ardently gripped by his repentance I calmed him down. Turning to the impatient crowd I told it that I had wholeheartedly pardoned him.

Despite the fact that I had very little cash left on me I gave Baga all I had. The dismayed mob murmured scornful words against the former commander before walking away.

I remained standing by the side of comrade Baga. I needed to know why he was crippled. Flustered and abashed he said the enemy jets bombed the guerrilla camp in Mozambique where he was in charge and fifty-seven people lost their lives in the incident. That happened about six months after my escape. During the barbaric assault a bomb shrapnel split his left leg from the knee. In agony he witnessed the fragments of his flesh thrown about four meters elsewhere. And he was treated by Ms. Marija at Chimoio. Deeply touched I comforted him as his plight was woeful.

Distraught by the catastrophic situation I suggested that he had to go to the Ministry of Social Welfare as it was responsible for looking after the destitutes and the crippled nationals. The ministry was also assigned to offer accommodation and upkeep allowances for indigent citizens. But he said he had seen the department and the officials were biased on where he came from. Consequently, he didn't get any help.

Looking pale, degenerated and frustrated, Baga said he had advanced prostate cancer. All his effort to be medicated had failed. Had I been employed I would had helped him financially. As well I would had looked for a medical institution that had the capacity to help him. However, I noted his phone number as I vowed to look around for a helper. Then I left him baffled and disturbed mentally.

CHAPTER 28

As I prearranged Ms. Marija and Mr. Gara cordially agreed to come to my home as soon as I returned from the varsity.

On the day I went to the Ministry of Health I had to meet the duo at the Harare International airport so that the three of us were to fly to Victoria Falls for a tour. Thereafter, we were to have a day's outing in the Wankie Game Park.

Our meeting at the airport was incredibly heartening. And, the flight to Victoria Falls or Mosi Oa Tunya (the smoke that thunders) in the local language, took about two hours. We hired a four-wheel drive double cab pickup shortly after landing at the resort airport. Then we proceeded to the majestic gorge.

The pounding force from the plunging water into the awesome ravine was intensely thunderous. And, the vibration from the flowing, massive volume of water was felt about three kilometers away. We were overwhelmed by the numerous rainbows which sparkled in the bright sunny sky.

The breath-taking magnificent falls spreads out for about 1.7 kilometers where the smoky spray rises way up into the atmosphere. The whole landscape was wreathed in a misty cover which showered the lush evergreen vegetation. We were soaked by the drizzle. And, to our astonishment we observed the European boys who were playing in the slippery, wet rock on the edge of the life-threatening 350 feet deep canyon. Passionately I boldly went and warned the juveniles to retreat to the safe ground as they were dicing with death. Ms. Marija sincerely acknowledged my swift action.

We eye witnessed the dangerous Bungee jump from the point above the falls which left us sighing. As well, we were captivated by the white water rafting downstream in the mighty Zambezi river.

Then we made a lateral turn to look at David Livingstone's statue. He was a Scottish Missionary who was the first European to see the falls in 1855. The local Africans called it the Mosi Oa Tunya. It was nightfall. Fairly exhausted we went to our booked hotel for dinner and sleep.

CHAPTER 29

Early in the morning we left Victoria Falls and traveled to Hwange National Park. Located north west of Zimbabwe. the Wilderness boasts of being one of the largest game parks in Africa and covers an area of 14 600 square kilometers. It is home to the renowned African Big five game; the lion, the elephant, the leopard, the buffalo and the rhinoceros. There are 199 mammal species including the following critically endangered animals; the wild dog, the black rhino, the roan and the sable. The national park brags of 50 000 elephants and 600 lions among the wide variety of species and abundant bird life.

The best time for game viewing at the man-made waterholes where the animals drink is in winter between July and October. And, we chose September as the ideal time for the sight-seeing event.

During our two hours' drive into the park's outskirts, we encountered a few lovely antelopes on either side of the road.

Enthusiastically we enjoyed to see some varieties of game in our tour. Then Ms. Marija parked the vehicle about fifty meters overlooking a forty-meter man-made dam which was surrounded by a bushy Savannah landscape. The first animals to arrive were the wildebeests. They were eighteen of them. We all remained seated in the car for the safety reasons whilst Ms. Marija took photos and videos. Almost all the animals stood on the edge of the waterhole as they drank the precious liquid except a careless calf which went to quench its thirst whilst standing in the reservoir. In a savagely violent force the young animal was viciously dragged into the deeper portion of the water totally immersing it. It never had a chance to resist or cry out in pain as the attacking power was overwhelming. The frightened herd panicked and went away. We were gripped by sympathy. About thirty minutes later the brutal crocodile killer munched the chunks of its kill when it raised its mouth above the water.

Later the giraffe and the kudu herds appeared on the scene. They drank the treasured liquid and left.

It was about noon when we envied to enjoy the comprehensive game viewing. In almost forty minutes we saw herds of elephants, warthog sounders, buffalo herds, two lion prides and several antelope species. A few hyena and jackal scavengers jealously feasted on a buffalo carcass. Yet seemingly hungry vultures curiously waited to strike any opportunity on the decaying meal.

About thirty minutes later we saw a parked white sedan car on the left side of the road. A Chinese guy was taking camera photos of a resting lion pride. The beasts which numbered about seven were thirty meters from the vehicle. The photographer was standing very close to the passenger's door facing the fierce animals. Ms. Marija parked her vehicle behind the Chinese automobile. Our compelling interest on the brutes was immeasurable.

Both groups in the vehicles were completely unaware of the rogue lioness which was sneaking and crawling along the vehicle sides. The devilish animal was targeting the cameraman. The diabolic beast must had come from a thick bush behind us.

All we saw was an abrupt, swift indescribable movement of the villain when it violently attacked the photographer. In anguish he yelled in vain. Scared in bone chilling fear and puzzlement we couldn't help him.

Sadly, we witnessed the innocent individual's dead body being picked by the varmint. Vehemently the other lions fleetly surrounded the kill, and they viciously fought among themselves for the possession of the human meat. In about twenty minutes he was voraciously devoured. It was an unbelievable sorry sight. Apprehensively the Chinese driver left for the national park office. Totally put off we consequently canceled our tour destinations, as we headed to the Victoria Falls airport ready to fly back to Harare.

On arrival in the capital city Ms. Marija and Mr. Gara were booked in a five-star hotel. Doubtlessly they needed a peaceful night rest. However, the following day the duo was scheduled to come to my home. And, hurriedly I left in a taxi going home to prepare for the dignitaries visit.

CHAPTER 30

Prior to the turning up of Ms. Marija and Mr. Gara, I had organized my associates to offer our visitors a cordial reception. Within half an hour our guests showed up.

Buttressed by the horde, the entertainment group jovially gave the honorable visitants a distinguished, and privileged treatment. It was a unique atmosphere deluged with jubilation which was ignited by sensational music and dancing in a cool, sunny afternoon. The barbecue team was not spared either. Their skill in roasting and preparing a sumptuous feast was second to none.

The assemblage had swelled more than our expectations. However, we then urgently prepared for the anticipated circumstance.

There was a marquee tent and adequate tables and chairs for the function. When the throng had settled, food was served by the youths. Whilst on the high table mouth-watering food was dished to us by a bevy of girls.

Shortly after the lavish banquet I had a bizarre feeling in my stomach. Repeated vomiting and severe watery bloody diarrhea developed. A high alarming temperature of 39⁰C, nausea and abdominal cramps followed. Ms. Marija gave me plenty of water to drink. But all was in vain. A fast heart beat and froth around my mouth were of great concern to me. She was frightfully shattered. My mum and Joe were alarmingly distressed at my condition too. What had I eaten?

Ms. Marija suggested to dash off with me to a Harare private medical institution for an urgent attention. Unquestionably my family agreed. We then concurred that I had to be carried in her vehicle with mum and Joe.

When we arrived at the medical establishment I wasn't able to speak properly. But I was capable to see what was happening. Promptly a medical specialist prescribed an intravenous rehydration to treat the severe dehydration. Abruptly I went into a coma. It was said that my mother collapsed in utter bewilderment. She was resuscitated hastily and got well.

CHAPTER 31

The following day my health had improved. Nevertheless, I was still having sharp, deep pain in my abdomen. And, two days later I felt better off. Speaking and eating liquid food was not a problem any longer. However, my pitfall baffled my mother who had not expected it. As she gazed at me sleeping in a hospital bed she whimpered whilst murmuring the following words: "Why ---? But --- why? Why Ziff --- were you --- dying in front --- of me? I --- love --- you --- my dear son ---!" She emitted a long, deep audible breath expressing sadness.

Though I was weak I managed to reply her. "Mum --- I --- didn't --- wish --- to die! Oh --- no! It --- just --- happened --- beyond --- my expectation."
Then she continued: "Do --- you --- know who --- poisoned --- you?"
I said: "I --- don't --- know, mum!"

After a pronounced recovery the physician discharged me from the establishment. The willing Ms. Marija drove me back home. There was a letter from the Ministry of Health. It ignited my high hopes of employment. Unfeigned I yearned to get the medical job.

Strikingly the written contents awfully distressed me. It was as follows:

"The Ministry of Health regrets to turn down your application as there are no doctor's vacancies at the moment.

Regards

R.I.P Godo
(The Permanent Secretary for the Ministry of Health.)"

Discomposed and stupefied I saw my high visions thwarted. For some moments I was disoriented with jumble and racing thoughts. Ms. Marija requested to see the distasteful letter. Regretfully she got despondent after reading it

CHAPTER 32

I fasted and prayed to God for three days. And, amazingly Ms. Marija recollected her close friend who was working as a physician in Canada. She then communicated with her bosom buddy, Jelena.

Likewise, Ms. Marija had taken a month's leave from her work and there was ample time to sort out my challenges. In a week's time the two tireless ladies worked hard. Thereafter, Ms. Jelena sent me comprehensive application documents which I filled in. Then I did send the information back to the institution in Canada.

Stupendously the combination of Ms. Marija and Ms. Jelena produced a greener pasture for me in the North American nation. The breakthrough was like a dream. In Jubilation I thanked the assiduous duo.

I was scheduled to fly to the tourist town of Vancouver in British Columbia to start an induction course in my medical career. I couldn't wait to go through the stepping stone into my health profession. Generously Ms. Marija gave me a loan to cover the anticipated expenses.

Before the expiry date of her leave days the luminary, dedicated Ms. Marija was urgently needed at her work in Mozambique. And, abruptly she hastily left accompanied by Mr. Gara. My family and I gave them our resounding, heartfelt farewell as we stood astounded and befuddled.

A fortnight later, just before I left Harare for Canada, I telephoned the former commander, Baga. There was no response. I was committed to assure him of my firm financial support in the foreseeable future if I worked in the North American nation. After an hour the commandant's wife returned my call. But sadly she said her husband had passed on after a long battle with prostate cancer. Thunderstruck and baffled I found my tears spontaneously tricking down my cheeks.

DISCLAIMER

Although the publisher and the author have made excessive efforts to bring perfect and accurate information contained in this book, we take no responsibility for mistakes and inaccuracies herein

THE END